DREAM FRIENDS

STORY & ART BY

You Byun

Nancy Paulsen Books ◯ An Imprint of Penguin Group (USA) Inc.

Once there was a girl named Melody,
and she had a very special friend . . .

. . . in her dreams.

Her friend could fly so fast!

He surprised her with lovely things.

They played hide-and-seek.

They watched fireworks.

They had fun together every day

and every night.

. . . but only in her dreams.

Melody was new in the neighborhood,
and she was too shy to talk to the other children.
She wanted her dream friend in her real world.

She tried to coax him out
from her dream,

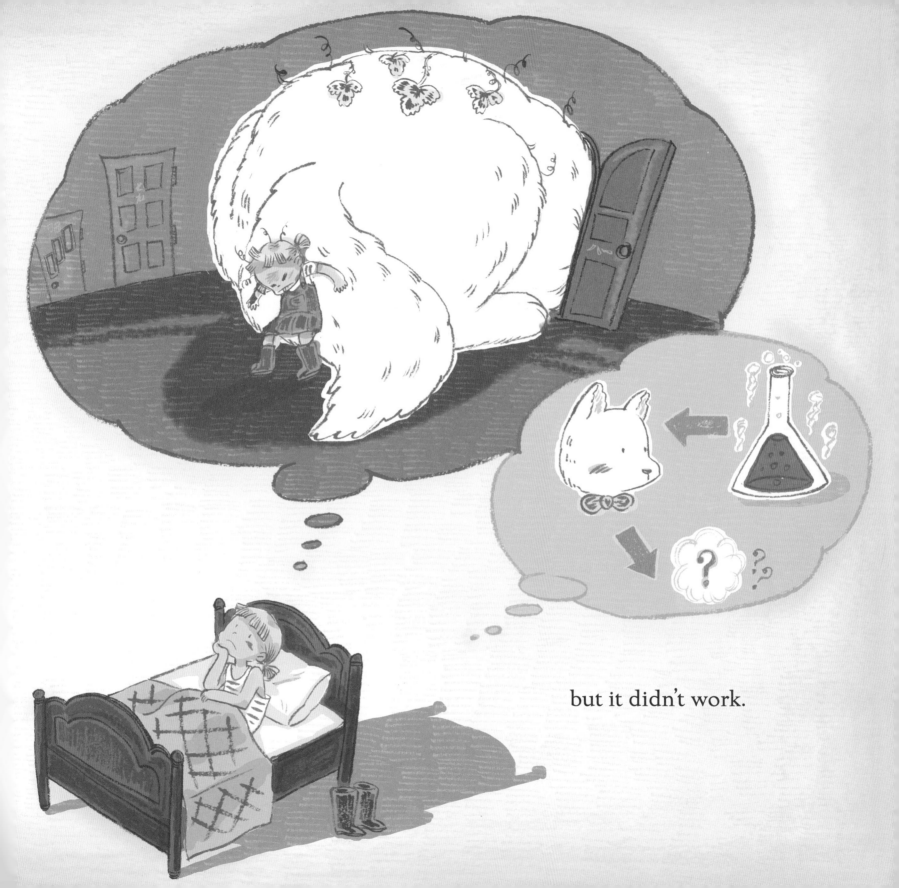

but it didn't work.

One day she was at the playground, feeling lonely.
She wished her friend was with her.

She thought about the fun they'd had in her dream the night before . . .

She closed her eyes.

She danced their dance.

She felt her friend was with her.

"Is that a new game?" someone asked.
Melody opened her eyes and saw a girl.

"Can I play with you?" the girl asked.
So Melody taught her the dance she learned from her friend.

Soon everyone on the playground
was dancing with them.

There was no magic like in her dreams, but it was . . . magical.

Melody's new friend wanted to meet Melody's dream friend.
So they had a sleepover.

Melody was hoping they could all have fun together.

And they did.

My first book is dedicated to who made this dream book come true:

my wonderful picture book mentor, children's book artist PAT CUMMINGS;

NANCY PAULSEN, who found this book and made a miracle happen—without her, this book wouldn't exist;

CECILIA YUNG, who art directed everything about this book with brilliant insights on art;

MARIKKA for the beautiful design for the book, and SARA for all the work and help;

art lovers and young talent supporters SOOJIN and CHRIS;

my teachers SUNGPYO, NAMI, MARSHALL, KIM, DAVID, CARL, MIRKO, CAROL,
GREG, COUCH, MATTHEW, MICHELLE & YUKO;

OZEE, BOO, HEESUN, HYUNAH, JUNGMIN, JI-EUN, THOMAS, ANDRÉ, JOJO, ANNA,
HAENA, HANE, KEVIN, DAISY, ANNIE & JON;

and lastly, to my parents and my sister, who taught me everything I know and everything I dream.

NANCY PAULSEN BOOKS • A division of Penguin Young Readers Group. Published by The Penguin Group.
Penguin Group (USA) Inc., 375 Hudson Street, New York, NY 10014, U.S.A.
Penguin Group (Canada), 90 Eglinton Avenue East, Suite 700, Toronto, Ontario M4P 2Y3, Canada (a division of Pearson Penguin Canada Inc.).
Penguin Books Ltd, 80 Strand, London WC2R 0RL, England.
Penguin Ireland, 25 St. Stephen's Green, Dublin 2, Ireland (a division of Penguin Books Ltd).
Penguin Group (Australia), 250 Camberwell Road, Camberwell, Victoria 3124, Australia (a division of Pearson Australia Group Pty Ltd).
Penguin Books India Pvt Ltd, 11 Community Centre, Panchsheel Park, New Delhi - 110 017, India.
Penguin Group (NZ), 67 Apollo Drive, Rosedale, Auckland 0632, New Zealand (a division of Pearson New Zealand Ltd).
Penguin Books (South Africa) (Pty) Ltd, 181 Jan Smuts Avenue, Parktown North 2193, South Africa.
Penguin Books Ltd, Registered Offices: 80 Strand, London WC2R 0RL, England.

Design by Marikka Tamura. Text set in Golden Cockerel ITC Std.
The art was created using paintbrushes and ink on watercolor paper, and then manipulated digitally.

Library of Congress Cataloging-in-Publication Data
Byun, You. Dream friends / You Byun. p. cm.
Summary: "A shy little girl yearns to find a real-life friend as wonderful as the one she plays with in her dreams"—Provided by publisher. [1. Imaginary playmates—
Fiction. 2. Dreams—Fiction. 3. Moving, Household—Fiction. 4. Friendship—Fiction.] I. Title. PZ7.B998Dre 2013 [E]—dc23 2012011082
ISBN 978-0-399-25739-1
3 5 7 9 10 8 6 4 2